To Michael

THE GOLEM OF PRAGUE

PREQUEL TO THE HIRAM KANE ACTION THRILLER SERIES

STEVEN MOORE

I hope you like it.

Cheers,

CONDOR PUBLISHING

PROLOGUE

"PLEASE DON'T HURT THE CHILDREN," PLEADED Judith Anderson, their teacher. "Please, they're just innocent kids."

The woman glared at her. "Shut up. Do as I say and they will not be hurt," the woman lied. "Just keep moving."

With her gun pointed directly at the children, the woman hustled the eight terrified middle school-aged children and their raven-haired teacher down the dark, damp corridor. They were somewhere deep beneath the walls of ninth-century Prague Castle. The kids were on a late afternoon field trip from their extra-curricula English Academy. Their teacher, Judith, had brought them to the castle for a little fun. She knew that beyond the confines of the classroom, these kids could excel. They had arrived deliberately late in order to avoid the day's crowds of flocking tourists, in what was one of the most popular sites to visit in the ancient, picturesque city.

What happened next was nothing short of a whirlwind of terror.

They were quietly exploring St. Vitus Cathedral, practicing their English with their teacher and in pairs with their friends. They'd all made their way over to a quiet corner of the nave, where they set about reading the engravings on the walls. As if from out of nowhere, a woman suddenly appeared. The woman wore a warm smile beneath small, some might say beady eyes. On her jacket was an official-looking badge that informed Judith she was a 'Cathedral Guide'. As she approached the group, she spoke in a kindly voice, first in flawless English with a hint of an accent, then Czech.

"Excuse me. Would the kids would like to visit the secret room? It is a room so secret, most of Prague's citizens have never even heard of it. It is a rare opportunity." She held Judith's eyes, smiling, while challenging her to deny the kids their chance.

"No tourists have ever been inside," she said,

adding a wink for good measure, trying to tempt the foreign teacher.

"Well, I don't know," Judith replied. It wasn't part of the strict schedule, and Judith Anderson was nothing if not a stickler for the rules. Yet, the kids had heard the offer from the guide. As one, they had chimed in with great enthusiasm. It was obvious they would all like to visit the mysterious room. Their vociferous pleas to their teacher grew in volume. She glanced around. The kids were drawing some unwanted attention from a group of snooty tourists. Rather than cause a scene, Judith reluctantly agreed. Besides, she loved a little adventure herself. The woman who had made the offer was an official guide of the cathedral, after all. *What harm can it do?* she mused.

"Okay then. Yes, please," she said. "We will take you up on your offer. *Děkuji*," she added. Thank you.

"Very good, Miss...?"

"Miss Anderson. Please, call me Judith."

The guide's eyes suddenly narrowed to slits. It were as if she had been personally insulted. She sucked in a sharp breath, and for a second it looked as if she might even bare her teeth. Somehow Judith missed the fearsome expression in the gloom of the cathedral. Using that same gloom to her advantage, the guide quickly recovered her composure.

"Well, *nemáš zač*, Judith. You are welcome." Again, Judith missed the derision in the woman's voice.

The guide offered a curt nod. Then she turned to the kids. "Okay, children. As promised, I will take you into the secret room. In return for this great privilege, you must also promise to be quiet. As I told you, it is so secret, we do not want everyone to learn about it, do we? Do you all agree?"

Each child nodded their assent. The guide smiled again. It was forced. *Easier than I thought*, she mused, *much easier*.

Moments later she was leading the students and their teacher toward a large statue in the very far corner of the expansive nave. In the shadows behind the statue, the guide showed them to a door. So concealed was the door, it could not be seen by anyone unless they already knew it existed there. Judith was surprised. She had been bringing students here on occasion for the last couple of years, and she had never before seen it.

From her pocket the guide produced a large key. A second later, she had deftly unlocked the ancient wooden door and stepped aside, demonstrating the darkness that lie beyond.

Judith was hit with a sudden rush of cool, damp air from the newly-opened door. A flutter of trepidation twisted in her gut. Sensing her concern, the guide stepped closer to her and spoke quietly.

"It is okay, Judith. Do not worry. This door does not get opened very often. It is totally fine." Next she turned to the children. Stepping behind them in order to corral them towards the door, she said, "Okay, which brave child wants to go first?"

But no sooner had she asked the question, the children, led by a bigger, tubby boy at the front, were disappearing through the doorway and away into the darkness.

Now, turning back to Judith, the guide smiled once more. "Well Judith, it doesn't looks like you have any choice now, does it? Come on. Let's go."

Judith returned the smile. Yet, she found she had to force it, and felt as if it were laced with a touch of something like fear. Inhaling deeply, she stepped through the low door and, against her better judgment, she followed after the children.

Judith had taken just a few steps into the damp corridor, when the guide swung the door closed behind them with a hefty thud. It instantly plunged them all into darkness. One of the girls screamed. The thick, ancient walls absorbed the sound. Suddenly a powerful torch flashed on, illuminating the old passage. Judith let out a breath of relief she hadn't realised she'd been holding.

"Okay everyone, let us move quickly and quietly along the tunnel," said the guide. Her face had taken on the appearance of a gargoyle beneath the dancing beams of the powerful torch. "Go. Now!"

She hustled her way past the kids to the front of the small procession. From there she urged them forward. "Come on, children, there is nothing to be afraid of. It is exciting, isn't it?"

Despite herself, Judith had to agree that it was indeed exciting. Much more fun than taking rubbings of the stones in the cathedral above. She recalled when her father used to take her to castles and dungeons while on holiday at home in England as a youngster. That thrill of being somewhere so ancient. Somewhere so many things had happened, and where historical kings and queens might just have treaded along these very same steps she was. Judith relished those memories. She decided to relish this moment too. Judith was glad her students were getting the chance to do the same. It's how memories were formed, she knew. As she relaxed and edged along the dark passageway, a thrill of excitement tingling in her guts, she hoped it would help foster in these kids the same adventurous spirit her father had fostered in her.

KANE

HIRAM KANE WAS IMAGINING THINGS.

At least, he thought he was. He looked back to check anyway. This time he saw nothing, other than the bobbing heads of hundreds of other tourists. Today, they were people just like him; travellers — foreigners, mostly — enjoying the historical sites and minding their own business. *Too many pints last night,* he mused, his trademark wry grin curling his lips as he turned and carried on toward the bridge.

The 14th-century Charles Bridge, allowing foot traffic across the river on the fringes of Prague's Old Town, was one of the busiest tourist traps in Europe. Kane usually tried his best to avoid such places, at least at peak times. Today though he was heading to an afternoon appointment, and crossing the beautiful bridge was his most direct route. Despite the thronging masses of anorak-wearing, map and mobile phone-wielding tourists, Kane was having fun.

And yet, although he hadn't really seen anyone suspicious, he sensed with unnerving certainty that he were being followed. At the very least, he sensed, he felt as if he were being watched. By whom, and why? Kane had no idea whatsoever. Nevertheless, he couldn't shake the eerie feeling, and subconsciously quickened his stride.

The quirky paranoia he felt today was unusual. Kane was a tough man, a rugged outdoorsy-type afraid of nobody or nothing. A lethal expertise in the Korean martial art of tae-kwon-do had helped develop his natural fearlessness over the previous decade and a half, since he'd first discovered a passion for the discipline, the respect and, he had to admit, the kick arse moves he'd mastered. Life had thrown plenty of danger Kane's way in recent years, and it had all helped to imbue in him a heightened awareness of what went on around him. It couldn't be called 'fear', not in the common use of the word. No, it were more a case of being ultra-prepared for the worst. The worst, as it happened, had played out far too often for his liking in recent times.

He was making a beeline across the city for Josefov, the former Jewish ghetto from centuries past. It was now home to the Jewish Museum. His old friend and mentor, Professor John O'nians, was in the city to conduct a seminar in the museum on the history of Jewish art and its antiquities. For O'nians it was part of a wider European speaking tour. It was the first of many scheduled seminars he'd be delivering in cities across Europe this autumn.

Kane had spent time in Prague before. He recalled at least two visits in the past — it might have been three, but Czech beer was notoriously strong. This trip, however, was to be his first time visiting that area of the city. Whenever he got the chance to attend the good professor's lectures, whatever subject they happened to be about, he took it. The professor was a legendary speaker, and for anyone who'd ever studied under the world-renowned scholar, more often than not, O'nians became kind of a cult hero, an inspiration for life. That's exactly how it was for Kane. As he hustled across the Vltava along the ancient, statue-lined Charles Bridge, he was excited to once more see his old friend in action.

Though he usually enjoyed the anonymity of the

crowds, and despite his innate reluctance for fame, Hiram Kane was globally known in certain circles. Now a world-renowned expedition leader based out of Cuzco, Peru, he had earned a reputation as one of the world leaders in his field. Added to that the fact his family name, Kane, was synonymous with adventure and exploration across the world, he would often get recognised. Yet, regardless of his keen eye and sharpened senses, Kane had somehow failed to spot the one person on the streets that day in Prague who knew who he was.

That man had been following Kane ever since he had left his hotel opposite the famous astronomical clock in Old Town Square, a clock that had been counting time for more than six-hundred years.

Kane didn't know it — couldn't have known it — but if he didn't give his pursuer what he wanted, Kane would be dead before the hands of that old clock had counted sixty more minutes.

O'NIANS

SOMETHING DIDN'T FEEL RIGHT.

Something was definitely off. What it was, Professor John O'nians didn't know.

"Surely not nerves," he muttered to himself. He knew it wasn't.

The professor had given thousands of presentations like the one that was due to kick off in half an hour. And, to much larger audiences. Although his specialty was the 'classics', and in particular the artistic and cultural histories of Greece and Rome, his peers nevertheless considered the revered art historian an expert on Jewish antiquities. It was exactly the reason he'd been invited to speak at this event. The name 'John O'nians', the organiser knew, could sell a lot of tickets.

The professor was as prepared as ever. Not that any listener could ever have doubted it. The truth was, O'nians never had any need for notes when he gave his presentations, and he never referred to books, not even his own, of which there had been many published, and to great acclaim. His phenomenal memory, and his uncanny ability to pluck knowledge and facts, seemingly from thin air and about any subject, was legendary. Many a student had felt disheartened with the professor, when he had apparently nodded off to sleep in his ancient leather swivel chair as they began presenting a daunting seminar. That disheartenment never lasted long. The moment they'd finished their presentations, the great man would spring from his chair with an athleticism belying his age, and surprise the entire class by asking an endless array of precise and detailed questions about the presentation. 'Flummoxed' would be a good way to describe how he left them feeling.

Hiram Kane himself had been undone by exactly that scenario when he'd studied beneath O'nians at university, what now seemed lifetimes ago.

The two men had been great friends — and

occasional colleagues — ever since. Each harboured enormous respect for the other's work.

This afternoon, as the autumn sun began to sink behind the mighty Prague Castle, and cast long shadows about the stones of the Jewish Cemetery, to the professor something felt decidedly off. Casting his eyes about the solemn graveyard, where he sat making last-minute mental-only notes on his presentation, O'nians at last smiled and shook his head. "Maybe I'm just getting old," he said to no one — or perhaps he said it to the twelve-thousand Jewish souls that had at one time or another lay buried there. Finally, he made his way back toward the museum to take up his position, front-and-centre, before commencing his much-anticipated speech.

O'nians was in fact getting old. He had officially retired a decade previous. However, such was his passion for teaching, and for the arts themselves, that he still thrived on life and relished his work. The professor remained as sprightly as a man half his eight decades.

As he stepped into the museum's rear entrance a pair of wild, yet narrowed eyes, followed his every move.

MAREK

Marek Fitz focused his eyes on the back of the man's head as he ducked in and out of the swarming humans crossing Charles Bridge.

Marek was satisfied with his job as a journalist — and part-time photographer — at the Prague Herald. Well, at least he believed he was... most of the time. He did enjoy exploring hidden corners of his home city, and he took the chance to get away from his desk as often as possible. His favourite part of the job, however, was digging up dirt on the dirtiest of politicians and so-called sports and pop stars. And yet...

When he really thought about it, Marek realised he was actually pretty fucking disillusioned with it all. The pay was no better than average. His chief editor was basically a bossy prick who wouldn't know a good story if it ran up and punched him on his big ugly Jewish nose. Marek didn't consider himself racist. He didn't hate Jews, especially. Just didn't like many of them. Especially his fucking boss.

Marek in fact was not satisfied with his job, nor with his lot in life overall. He needed many things. He needed his ego stroked. He needed a big story. He needed to get fucking laid. In terms of his job, though, he needed a story that would give his career the boost it needed, while at the same time wiping the smug smirk off his editor's fat face. A few weeks ago it had dawned on Marek Fitz what he needed to do. And although it might prove risky, he figured it was worth taking the chance.

A couple of weeks before that he had met a woman called Magda. They had met in a bar, and though he was about ready to bite the bullet and pay to bang one of the hookers peddling their fleshy wares around Wenceslas Square on any given night, this chick was sexy. The fact she had taken the time to chat him up was the first surprise. The second surprise was that he actually liked her. Magda was a mysterious woman, whom had both fascinated him and yet, in a strange way, had somehow scared him.

Though he couldn't pinpoint why that was at that time, there was something about her that kept him on edge. She was smart, no doubt, and pretty — too pretty for him, he knew that too. There was just a certain devilment about her that intrigued him. Marek's record with the opposite sex was at best average. So, when he'd been what he believed was 'chatted up' by Magda in the bar that night, he had almost run a mile.

Yet, she mentioned something to him over drinks that night that had aroused his curiosity, as well as his manhood. She simply stated that, very soon, there would be an event in Prague which would shake the ancient city to its crumbling foundations. Furthermore, she said that if he wanted to be a part of the biggest story the city had witnessed in decades, he just had to help her achieve something. The details of what that something was were vague. He dismissed it initially as nothing more than drunken chatter. But, before the night was over she had detailed a specific date, and something about some treasure, and a name... Karl, or Kane, or something like it. After that, Marek's interest had been piqued enough that it had remained in his thoughts weeks later.

Over the following days he had set about doing

a little research. He learned that there was soon to be an important seminar given by a world famous art historian. Marek Googled the name. He learned that an Englishman, a Professor John O'nians, was to speak at the event. A little more research informed Marek that O'nians was involved somehow with the explorer — some people might have called him a treasure hunter — Hiram Kane.

Hmm... an art historian and a treasure hunter? Here in Prague? On the same date?

Marek suddenly needed to know more. That evening he would call Magda. He wanted in. Whatever it was, Marek Fitz wanted in. He would get his fucking story. Maybe he'd get laid at the same time.

He called the mysterious Magda Pokorna on the number she'd left him on a bar coaster that night. She explained to Marek what she wanted. "It is simple," she said. "I just need you to follow Mr. Kane from his hotel on the day of the seminar."

"That's it?" Marek asked, dubious. "Just follow him?"

Magda paused, as if to tease Marek. Then she said, "That all depends on what you want."

"What do you mean, what I want? What are you talking about?" *Is she insane?* he wondered.

"I mean, do you only want a story? Or do you want..." The enigmatic Magda paused again.

Marek had never been known for his patience. "Or do I want what?"

She smiled to herself, a conspiratorial gleam in her dark eyes. Marek of course couldn't see either. Magda exhaled, the line crackling a little. "Or, do you want to become richer than you could ever imagine?"

MAGDA

MAGDA LIT ANOTHER CIGARETTE AND TOOK another long look at herself in the mirror.

She liked what she saw. It's not that she cared that she was pretty. Others seemed to think it was true. She was inclined to agree with them. It's more that she was proud of herself for what she had become. Other people wouldn't really understand it. She knew that. That didn't matter. Some lesser humans would never know what was good for them.

Magda knew she was on a mission. That mission was a legacy passed down through many generations, stretching back at least a century since the great man himself had forever changed the face of Europe. Or, at least, he had tried to. He was succeeding, until other, less cultured and less wise men had stopped him. Nevertheless, she felt sure he would be proud of her. He *was* proud of her. He had been honoured his rightful place in the history books. One day that honour would also be hers.

He had been dead more than half a century. Yet, many folks still felt his influence, and in many places, not least in the run-down cities of Central and Eastern Europe. He was known as The Führer back then. The Leader. In her mind, he was the greatest human that had ever lived. He was still her leader. His work was unfinished. She had picked up that mantle. She would continue his noble cause, and she was doing it with ice in her veins and steel in her heart.

To continue his great and noble work, however, Magda needed funds. Her brilliant and beautiful plan to secure those funds was about to enter its final stage.

She'd recruited a local journalist to help. She wasn't one hundred percent convinced of his dedication to the plan — of course, he didn't know all the crucial details. She did know he was weak, stupid, and desperate for recognition in his field of journalism. If he held up his end of the bargain, he would definitely get the fame — and the notoriety

— he so craved. The fact he wouldn't live long enough to enjoy it was of no concern to her.

She took one final glance at herself in the mirror, mentally preparing for the final stage of her plan to secure those vital funds. Magda knew that she herself, as well as that limp-dick Marek Fitz, were just unimportant pawns in the bigger game. It was a game that started when Anton Drexler and Karl Harrer came together in 1918. The result of that meeting between those wondrous, collaborative minds, was what became known as the Nazi party, so ably and brilliantly led by the magnificent genius of Adolf Hitler.

Magda took a deep breath and touched up her lipstick a final time. She tilted her head a fraction to the left. "I am pretty," she whispered. She took a last drag on her cigarette before dropping it to the floor of her bathroom and stamping it out beneath her heel.

Magda turned and picked up her handbag from a chair. She looked inside to make sure everything was secure. Once satisfied, she shrugged on her black leather jacket and stepped out into the cool mid-afternoon sun. She was ready.

She whistled as she walked. If she had sung the

words to the song, however, it would have gone something like this:

When Jewish blood splashes from the knife,
Hang the Jews, put them up against the wall,
Heads are rolling, Jews are hollering.
When Jewish blood splashes from the knife...

THE SEMINAR

AN HOUR LATER EVERYTHING WAS IN PLACE.

Magda watched from the shadows as the old professor made his way into the auditorium. A moment later she followed, ready to take her place in the front row. If things went to her plan, Marek Fitz would be within yards of Hiram Kane as the professor's friend also took a seat prior to the seminar starting.

Magda and Marek were armed. Marek was reluctant, but Magda insisted if he didn't comply he was out. She doubted the lame journalist would actually have the balls to use his gun. She also doubted he'd need to. She wouldn't hesitate to use hers, of course. Then again, if things went to plan there would be no need to kill O'nians or Kane.

She truly didn't care if either man lived or died. However, the professor was about to deliver a presentation regarding the alleged beauty of Jewish art and treasures on show within the museum. In other words, that meant he admired them. Which in turn, she knew, meant he was a Jewish sympathiser. *Perhaps I'll kill him anyway,* she mused, *as a kind of bonus for his appreciation of Jewish... of all the disgusting Jewish things.*

Magda involuntarily shuddered as she stepped across the threshold into the museum. Fucking Jewish filth made her skin crawl. Of course, most people attending this bullshit would be creatures of that despicable race. Still, she had work to do. She trailed the professor toward the front of the auditorium, then watched as he took his place behind the podium.

There were still fifteen minutes before the presentation was due to begin. The large room was slowly filling up. She shivered again, but not from the coolness of the room. It was knowing she would soon be surrounded by dirty, stinking Jew pigs.

Magda put the abhorrent thought out of her mind and focused on the task at hand. If her idol, the mighty, wondrous Adolf Hitler could do it, all for the greater good, then so could she. She would not fail.

She glanced over her shoulder, just in time to see Hiram Kane walk into the room. He paused and glanced about for a moment, appraising the room, then grinned as he approached the professor at the front. Moments behind Kane, Marek walked in and glanced in her direction. The pair locked eyes. The journalist looked nervous. He tipped Magda an almost imperceptible nod, then stood off to the side, busying himself with his camera equipment. It was part of the ruse, while he waited to see where Kane would sit.

Kane and Professor O'nians shared a warm hug, then began chatting amicably, like the old friends they were. Magda could tell in an instant they were close. She knew that would work in her favour. *Nothing like using the weakness of human emotions to get what you want,* she thought, and afforded herself a brief smile. *This is going to be easy.*

AFTER CHATTING FOR A FEW MINUTES, Kane wished his old friend good luck. Then he took his place on a seat in the front row. He had promised O'nians he wouldn't heckle. He didn't promise he wouldn't try to catch him out with a difficult question or two. John accepted the challenge. Both men knew there would only ever be one winner.

Not that John O'nians needed luck, of course. He was a master at delivering presentations, and his unmatched knowledge in the realms of art history was world famous. In fact, when Kane was a student under the professor at the University of East Anglia many years ago, once a week John would fly west across the Atlantic to one Ivy League university or other to give a presentation. He would fly back again the same night. The man was immensely popular, and his scholarly genius was sought after at establishments across the globe.

In their brief chat, John had just informed Kane he had agreed to conduct a lecture series in China the following semester. *I hope I have half the energy he has when I'm that age,* Kane thought. He smiled as he settled back into the uncomfortable wooden chair.

A moment later, a big guy sat down next in the chair beside him. Kane thought that was odd, since there were dozens of empty seats all around him. *Cosy*, Kane mused. He turned and said hello.

"Hello," the big man replied, and smiled. However, the smile was soon replaced by an awkward stare. After Hiram Kane met the odd stare in kind, the man quickly averted his eyes.

Hmm, weird. Kane then turned, slightly baffled as he reminisced about his university days. Hiram Kane loved art. As a student under O'nians, he had enjoyed all genres of art history. Despite his eclectic tastes, his main focus centred on the 'field of archaeology', a crap play on words he'd said to his friends far too often. If he were being honest, he only chose to select the professor's classes to be around the professor himself. In Kane's mind, O'nians was far and away the most interesting lecturer on any of his courses. Looking back, he was glad of his choices. The two men were now firm friends.

He never actually completed his education. After graduating from his bachelor degree — the result of a monumental effort from Kane, quick to admit he would never be a natural academic — he had quit just before completing his masters'. Back then he claimed he much preferred going out to discover things rather than just sitting around talking about them. He hadn't regretted it for a single second since.

However, in truth Kane knew little or nothing about Jewish art, nor cared much for it. He was really only there in Prague to catch up with his friend and pick his brains about an upcoming trip. After the seminar was over, and once the traditional drinks and the mingling with the crowd had finished, Kane was taking O'nians out for dinner. He wanted discuss his own plans with his friend and mentor. Kane was soon to head to Japan for a speaking engagement. Public speaking was not his strong suit, and there was no one better than to ask advice about public speaking that Professor John O'nians.

MAREK FITZ HAD NEVER BEEN SO FAR out of his comfort zone. Right now he was enduring a wave of second thoughts about what he'd agreed to do for Magda Pokorna. His role was meant to have been simple. He'd been instructed, upon Magda's signal, to remove his gun from his bag and take Hiram Kane hostage. She had assured him it would all be over in a few seconds, and that no one would have to get hurt. She explained that she had access to a secret tunnel that led away from the seminar room. Once they were into that tunnel, she told him, it was impossible for them to get caught. Magda had promised Marek this was to be the most difficult part of the operation. Then, soon after, she told him she would reveal exactly what it was that would give him the story, and the fame, he was so desperate for.

"You'll be a hero," she had lied. "A national fucking hero. A hero to millions of your country-men, and to millions more across all Europe and beyond." The passion he saw in her eyes when she had said those words had convinced Marek she was sincere. Though he couldn't even hazard a guess as to what it was all about, he was hooked. He would do what she asked.

Marek knew he was a good journalist who deserved fame and recognition for his investigative and writing abilities. His skills were simply being stifled in a dying industry that no longer cared for the truth. Instead, he was tasked with supplying only tabloid bullshit that meant nothing to anyone but the owners and editors, who sold shitty papers and got rich from it. Meanwhile, the reporters and photographers got nothing, and the idiots buying the papers got ripped off.

He had struggled for long enough.

It was Marek's turn to spend some time in the limelight.

As he stole a glance to his left now, however,

his reservations caused his instincts to quiver. This Hiram Kane fucker was a big man, at least as tall as Marek. Leaner and stronger too, for sure. When their eyes had met a moment ago, Marek saw in Kane someone fearless, someone who had known hardship... no doubt, he was a tough fucking man!

Marek had reported on the wars in the Balkans. He had interviewed and photographed hardened soldiers, and victims, those who had lost everything to violence and greed. He had seen the pain and suffering in their eyes. This man Hiram Kane had those same eyes. It scared Marek. This would not be as easy as he'd been led to believe.

Marek's hand slid involuntarily to his camera bag. Slipping it inside, he felt the heft of the loaded gun. It made him feel better. A little. Anyway, it was too late now. He was committed.

And for some unknown reason he couldn't fathom, Marek feared the diminutive Magda Pokorna as much as he now feared Hiram Kane.

THE GOLEM OF PRAGUE

THE FLAMBOYANT EMCEE TOOK THE STAGE.

"Ladies and gentlemen," he said, "It is my great honour to present to you today such an esteemed art historian. He is a man who knows so much that he has forgotten more about the history of art than the rest of us put together have ever learned. So, without any further ado, joining us all the way from Norwich, England, would you please welcome the revered scholar, Professor John O'nians."

The tuxedoed emcee stepped aside, as the gathered crowd of close to three hundred people welcomed John O'nians with a generous round of applause. The world-renowned professor, as humble as ever, swooshed his hands to quiet them. With a warm and grateful smile, John launched into his presentation.

"*Děkuji*," he said. "Thank you so very much. It is my great pleasure to have been invited to speak to you this afternoon, and in such a beautiful establishment. Our talk today will quite rightly focus on Jewish art, and its meaningful, important impact on the world of art as a whole, stretching back thousands of years to one of the great champions of art, King Solomon himself. But first, let me ask you a question. Who here has heard of the Altneuschul, or the Old-New Synagogue, situated just around the corner from here?" John watched as most of the audience raised an arm. "Very good," he said. "Very good. Now, did any of you know it's the oldest synagogue in Europe? And, were you aware that it dates back as far as the thirteenth-century?"

This time only a couple of hands rose in the crowd. A murmur of surprise rose instead. John smiled.

"And, my friends, have you seen those two beautiful columns?" He pointed to the green behind him. Even though he knew it was old-school, John still enjoyed a good old Powerpoint presentation. "They are almost certainly references to the two pillars that stood in front of King Solomon's

Temple, circa 900BC. They are known as Jachin and Boaz. Did anyone know that?" He paused. No hands at all this time. "Some people believe the building itself is constructed from the exact stones that formed the actual temple of the King."

Almost silence. As Kane might have said, *crickets*. Now John had the attentive crowd rapt, he was in his element.

The gathered guests sat enthralled, as they always were when John O'nians gave a presentation. Kane had sat through dozens of the professor's brilliant seminars, but they never got old. Such was John's deep, extensive knowledge, and his innate ability to add intrigue and humour to his talks, he somehow managed to pull off the notoriously difficult feat of both educating and entertaining in equal measures. Kane had no doubt that once the seminar was over, John's evocative words would have created many more passionate art historian hobbyists from within this crowd. And, of course further inspiring those already studying the arts to do so with renewed energy and passion. O'nians was an inspiring man. Kane loved him for it.

John's presentation whizzed by in a blur of informative stories and anecdotes. To the smiling crowd, he said, "And so, my friends, thank you very, very much for listening."

The emcee once more made his way onto the stage. It was no surprise to Kane when all bar none of the crowd stood to applaud the professor. He had seen such a reaction many times before and knew it was nothing more than John O'nians' presentations deserved. After a couple of minutes the crowd settled. The emcee returned to the front.

"Wow, wasn't that great?" he asked. The question was undoubtedly rhetorical. "Okay, everyone. Thank you for your warm applause. We have about fifteen minutes for you to ask the professor your questions. Please, raise your hands if you have something you want to ask our brilliant expert."

Immediately, a flurry of hands shot up. The emcee pointed to a young man a few rows back. "Yes, you sir, in the blue blazer. What would you like to ask?"

The man stood. "Thank you, and thanks, Professor, for a great presentation. My question is this..."

The Q and A session ran a full forty-five minutes past the scheduled stop time. O'nians' tireless enthusiasm remained unabated throughout, and was as well-known as his near magical memory.

Finally, the emcee had to intervene. "Okay, one last question. Who wants to ask it?"

A short woman in the front row stood up. She took a step forward. She had blonde, almost white hair, cut short. Her pretty, yet somehow harsh face sat on a slender neck protruding from a long black leather jacket. Kane hadn't noticed her before. The big man in the seat next to him suddenly sat upright and fidgeted in his chair. Kane observed the man's hands twitching in his lap. It was as if he were nervous.

The woman took another step forward. Then another, until she stood just a few yards from the professor. She looked around at the crowd. Her eyes settled for a moment on the big man sat next to Kane. She locked eyes with him for a long moment. Kane glanced to his left in time to see the man nod in her direction. His Adam's pale bobbed profusely.

These two know each other, Kane thought. Something about it didn't feel right. A shiver of apprehension caused the hairs on the back of his neck to stand up. *What's going on?*

"Yes, I have a question for you, Professor O'nians."

"Please, fire away," John replied.

"Why is it that you have opted to leave out the

most important information about this institution, and about the art on display here?"

O'nians' smile faltered for just a second. He was taken aback by the surprisingly forthright question.

"I... I'm not sure I understand your meaning, young lady. What did I leave out?" His smile returned. O'nians was rarely challenged about his knowledge, and he didn't think he had missed anything.

The woman glanced around at the crowds again and paused. An intrigued hush settled over the seminar room.

John's eyebrows furrowed. "I'm sorry," he asked again, now a little uncomfortable. "I'm not sure I understand the point. I —"

Kane sat upright in his chair. He looked on as O'nians flinched at the podium. *What on earth is this woman playing at?*

"I'm sorry, please repeat your question, Miss...?"

"My name is unimportant, Professor." She stepped forward again, and then took another short pace. She cast a quick glance back at Marek, who was now sitting upright in his seat. "What you have failed to tell these... these people... is the real reason the Prague synagogue has such a vast collection of Jewish art. Shall I tell them, Professor? Or would you like me to enlighten them?" She smiled, yet O'nians sensed malice in her dazzling blue eyes.

The truth was, John did know the real reason for the magnificent collection. It was not a good reason, definitely not a reason he wanted to share with the people in this audience.

"I... I really don't think there's any need to —"

"Don't worry, Professor O'nians," she interrupted, "I will save you the trouble." She turned, and angled her body to face the crowded room, while keeping O'nians in her peripheral vision. Kane sat up a little further. He was unsure quite what was happening, but something intangible had put his senses on high alert.

The woman seemed to have grown a little in stature. She raised her voice now, so no one missed a word. "The true reason the Prague synagogue contains such an enormous collection of Jewish art is because the Nazis had a plan. After they had exterminated all the Jews... every last one of the stinking pig Jews, which they would have succeeded in doing so if it were not for the ignorance of others... they were going to turn the museum into an exhibition of their extinct, repulsive Jewish culture!" She grinned widely now as a murmur of shocked discontent suddenly arose in the room. Then, as quick as a flash, she reached into her handbag and shocked everyone further. They all sat now in stunned silence as the woman levelled a gun at Professor O'nians' head.

Kane reacted fast, but he wasn't fast enough. Even before he could stand, the man sat next to him had leapt up and now held a gun. It was aiming right between his eyes.

"Do not move, Mr. Kane," the big man said. "Keep still, and no one will get hurt. Do not make me shoot you."

Kane tensed, his senses on fire at the unexpected danger. He gritted his teeth, eyes wide with anger. Hc exhaled through his nose, nostrils flaring with sudden rage at the two gun-wielding criminals, or whatever the hell they were. His knuckles turned white under the strain of his clenching fists. He knew it was too dangerous to attack the man. With all the innocent people sat around them, he couldn't risk one being accidentally shot. Or deliberately, for that matter.

Kane took a step back and nodded at the man. Marek's eyes never left Kane's.

"Professor O'nians, I do not wish to hurt you, nor anyone else in this room," the woman said. It was a practised lie. She had a plan. "So, if you do as I say, and if your friend Mr. Kane also does what I ask, then no one gets hurt. Do you understand?"

O'nians was visibly shaken. He had just given a presentation on the beauty and cultural importance of Jewish art, and now he was being threatened at gunpoint by a woman who was apparently a Neo-Nazi. John cast his eyes at his friend Hiram, mortified that he too had a gun pointed at him. He looked back at the woman, whose eyes bore into his like icy daggers. She meant business, he could tell by the steely look in her eyes and the impossibly calm, almost amused expression on her face.

"Who the hell are you?" he finally asked.

The woman stared at him as she pondered her answer. Then she smiled. "Professor O'nians, as far as you and these Jew pigs are concerned, I am the new Golem of Prague."

THREATS

"WHAT THE HELL ARE YOU DOING? THESE ARE innocent people."

An enraged John O'nians could hardly contain his anger. His surprise had well and truly worn off. Now he was furious. "How dare you —"

He fell silent when a gunshot split the air. Marek had fired his pistol into the ceiling, and it caused dozens in the audience to scream. And yet, no one had dared run. Instead, everyone had simply frozen on the spot.

Just two yards from Marek, Kane seethed. He was desperate to take the man down. He knew he could do it in seconds. He was just too afraid of the consequences. So, he decided to bide his time.

The woman's smile was unnerving. Cold.

Callous. Determined. "Like I said, Professor, no one here needs to get hurt. I have a few things I need you to do, along with your friend over there. If you comply, and only then, I see no reason why anyone here needs to die." Magda didn't yet feel the need to inform the men she had a load of school kids locked up like animals in a dungeon a hundred yards beneath where they now stood. They were her security, her insurance back up. If those little shits had to die for her cause, then die they would. Besides, they were Jewish kids. The very future of the scum race. They deserved to die like the animals they were. Perhaps she'd just kill them anyway. For fun. A lot of fun.

She knew that if he could see her now, the Führer would be pleased.

"So, will you help me with what I ask? Or do I have to shoot someone?" She nodded at Marek, who promptly swivelled and pointed his gun at a young woman standing next to Kane. The woman flinched, and it was all Kane could do to stop himself launching at Marek. He knew he could take him down — Kane imagined one swift roundhouse kick to the throat — but it was too risky. He didn't yet know the man's capabilities. Kane had underestimated people before with dire consequences. Again, he would wait.

"What do you want me to do?" asked O'nians.

"Oh, it is nothing much really. Not for a man... for men," — she nodded at Hiram — "of your combined capabilities. In fact, Professor, I believe you might even enjoy it."

"What the hell are you talking about?"

"Let's just say that you will need your skills, and Mr. Kane's prowess, in order to get me what I want."

"And what is it that you want?" O'nians asked. He didn't even try to hide the contempt from his voice.

Magda glared at him a long moment. Her eyes like ice picks into his soul. The smile never left her lips. "I want what all proud Aryan woman want..." She paused, and suddenly turned to face Hiram Kane. "You will convince your friend over there, Mr. Kane, to give me the money he stole from the jungles of Peru."

John O'nians almost choked. Kane actually laughed out loud, though he quickly stifled it. Once he composed himself, he said his first words since the drama began.

"I did not steal any money. I donated Atahualpa's gold to the Peruvian government. I do not —"

Marek suddenly thrust his gun under Kane's jaw, digging hard into the flesh of his throat. Magda moved quickly too and stepped toward him. "Mr. Kane, now is not the time for games. I know you received a reward of several million dollars from the government of Peru." She looked around at the horrified audience. "For those who don't know this man, he is Hiram Kane. Famous explorer. The reward was for locating the lost Inca city and its lost hoards of gold. Congratulations of finding that by the way. Impressive. But, now you are going to give it to me."

Despite her words, Magda knew all about the Kane family's unrivalled charitable work. She doubted there was any money left. That was okay. It was just a part of her ploy. She continued. "I understand several children died on that expedition, while under your control. I am sure their deaths haunt you still..." She let that truism hang in the air like a foul stench.

Kane's head dropped. Several people had died on his ill-fated expedition into the Andes Mountains. Some of them were kids. Though he wasn't directly responsible for their deaths, he still shouldered all the blame. He had never forgiven himself. He doubted he ever could.

Seeing Kane suffering, and enjoying it, now was the moment for Magda to play her hand. "I sense I am right about the guilt you feel. I am also sure you do not want another nine deaths on your hands. Do you, Mr. Kane?"

Kane's head shot up. Guts fluttering. Suddenly fearful. "What do you mean?"

She smiled, and it was that vicious, cruel smile again. "Listen very carefully. I have imprisoned eight Jewish children... and their Jew-whore teacher. They will die today. They will die, that is, unless my demands are met. It is very simple."

Money had no value to Kane. He didn't need it, and he had tried hard to decline the reward from the Peruvian state. They had insisted, reminding him what he did with the reward was of no consequence to them. Reluctantly, he accepted the vast amount. Since then, he had used every last penny of it to set up several charities in Peru, and other countries where children suffered. There was literally nothing left of that reward fund available to him. He guessed any money he might possess in his normal life would not be enough to satisfy this psychopathic woman.

And yet, he did not want to put any innocent lives at risk. Kane knew he would have to play along with her for now. "I can't... I can't get you that money. I need time."

Magda had expected this answer. It wasn't a problem. "Then, Mr. Kane, I recommend you come up with another idea to satisfy my desires. My whims. Like, for example, stealing one of the priceless artefacts on display within this city."

"I am not a thief," Kane spat. "How am I supposed to steal anything without getting caught? What you're asking is impossible."

"For most men, I would probably have to agree," she said, almost purring. "But not you. You will find a way, Mr. Kane, I am certain of it. Indeed, I imagine you always do."

JUDITH ANDERSON SHIVERED, not just from the cold, but from acute fear. She had been trussed in icy metal chains. Her hands were bound tight, and forced up behind her back. The chain was attached to a cleat set high in the stone wall. She couldn't move, and her legs were numb with cramps. Worse than that, she couldn't see a thing in the total darkness.

Her own condition was the least of her concerns. She was in charge of eight of her students. They too were tied up and suffering in the darkness. They too were afraid and cold and helpless.

How had this happened? What even is this? It was almost surreal. One minute they had been innocently making etchings of ancient carved scripts in the cathedral above. The next moment they were being ushered at gunpoint like cattle down the dark and damp tunnel. Then they were tied up like beasts in these cages. In fact, they weren't cages. They were medieval dungeons. Dungeons held prisoners. Judith knew that's exactly what they now were; prisoners.

Judith feared the worst. The woman who had abducted them was frightening. It wasn't her size or strength; she was a diminutive woman, a little over five feet tall. Barely a hundred pounds wet through. No, not her size. It was the look in her eyes. Eyes had bored into Judith's with such vitriol. Though it were for just a few seconds, Judith knew she wasn't bluffing. She felt certain the woman was capable of anything, including murder. Although she didn't know what the woman wanted overall, based on her obvious rage when she'd learned her name —

Judith, meaning *'woman of Judea'* — Magda had convinced her she was soon to become a victim.

Is she a Nazi? Judith wondered. *What do they call them? Neo-Nazis?*

Judith knew well that Neo-Nazism was on the rise across Europe, especially since the ever-growing influx of Arabs and Muslims from North Africa and the Middle East. The upsurge in racial friction had seen plenty of so-called 'skin heads' come out of the woodwork during her time living and working in Prague. Ironically, she wasn't actually Jewish herself. She just happened to work at a Jewish school teaching English. In fact, she had no religious affiliations at all. In truth Judith, despite her name, thought religion as a whole was just a little bit silly.

The school paid her better than most other academies at which she'd worked. She loved the kids she taught, and her bosses looked after her. They had given her the chance to fulfil her dream of living in Prague, a city she considered the most fairy tale-like in of all Europe.

The kids. Thinking of them all now, quivering in fear in the darkness, stirred something inside Judith. Suddenly, her silent tears stopped flowing. She shuffled a bit, and tried to sit a little more upright.

Judith knew she wasn't at fault for their kidnapping. She wasn't yet sure why they had been taken. But, she suspected the kids were to be used as a ransom or bargaining chip for a greater prize. No, this wasn't her fault.

Yet, they were her students. In that moment Judith Anderson resolved to do everything — anything — she could to get them to safety.

DEMANDS

"THOSE ARE IMPOSSIBLE DEMANDS," KANE SAID. "There is simply no way I can —"

Marek fired another shot. This time it slammed into the ground at the terrified woman's feet, and this time she screamed and started to run, stumbling over her chair.

Marek glanced at Magda. Calmly, she said, "Shoot her."

Marek was no killer. She had known it. She was prepared. Sensing his hesitation, Magda raised her own pistol. She stepped forward, took aim, and without blinking she shot the woman in the head. The woman slumped to the floor in a heap. The whole room stared in absolute shock at the fallen innocent, as a pool of crimson blood spread out around her head, turning the carpeted floor black. Magda's breathing remained even. Her pulse didn't miss a beat.

"You're insane!" O'nians shouted. "She's an innocent woman. Why did you need to kill her?"

"Professor, I just had to make sure I had your full cooperation. I needed to be certain that you take me seriously. I am not afraid to kill, Professor. You should heed my warning. You all should." She grinned, glancing down at the slain woman. "Perhaps now you have, hey? Anyway, as I said, I have eight children and their teacher secured somewhere they will never be found. In your eyes, they are innocent. That is not how I see it. Any Jew is, by default, guilty of crimes against humanity. In my eyes they all deserve to die. Every last one of them. However, they will live if you and Mr. Kane do as I ask. If you do not, they will starve and die and rot. Their corpses will remain undiscovered for all eternity. I care little. You, however? I suspect you do care. So..." — She looked at both Hiram and the professor in turn, before settling her hypnotic blue eyes back on O'nians — "Will you help me?"

Kane and John O'nians shared an agonised look.

They appeared to be helpless. The woman and the big man near Kane had guns. Though Kane sensed the man wasn't prepared to use his, they both knew the woman would use hers without pause. She had already slain one victim in cold blood. They had to believe she was capable of slaying more.

Kane inhaled deeply. His mind raced. *Who the hell is this woman? What the fuck do they really want?* He couldn't know. But he felt helpless, and though it pained him to do so, he complied. "I will help you," he said quietly. No one else needs to die."

"I am sorry, Mr. Kane, could you repeat that. Louder."

"I said I will help you. Just tell me what to do."

"I will help you too," said O'nians. He looked again at Kane. Hiram had his eyes fixed on the professor's. John noticed Kane's almost imperceptible nod, so subtle no one else in the room saw it. Not even Magda.

The professor had known Hiram Kane a long time, close to two decades. If he knew nothing else about the man, John knew Kane was a tough man with an unerring aptitude for getting things done. And John knew that, in that single, subtle nod, Kane was telling him he had a plan to put an end to this crazy drama.

If anyone could take control and lead the innocent young kids and their teacher to safety, the professor knew, then it was Hiram Kane.

THE LEGEND

"We will help you. First, you must let these people go," demanded O'nians, crisp authority in his voice, despite the threat of the guns. "This does not involve them."

"You are right, Professor." Magda turned slowly to the crowd, pointing her gun at them, stopping on individuals and aiming directly at them while grinning. "You are free to go. But be warned... if any of you reports this to the police, you should know that the deaths of the eight kids and their teacher will also be on your hands. I promise you now... if the police or any security comes looking for me, I will kill those fucking kids. Every one of those Jew bastards will die. It will be a slow and very painful death. No one will ever find their stinking bodies. Now, go!"

Immediately, the three hundred guests hustled out of the rear doors of the auditorium, scrambling for safety, terrified of being shot dead. Killed, like the innocent woman just moments ago. Herself the only one to know she was two months pregnant. Not a single one of the fleeing crowd doubted this mad woman would carry out her threat. Within thirty seconds the room had emptied. The only people left now were John O'nians, Hiram Kane, Marek Fitz, and Magda, the woman who had proudly called herself the Golem of Prague.

The name meant nothing to Hiram when he'd heard it. O'nians, on the other hand, knew exactly to what it referenced. The knowledge filled him with fear.

Back in the sixteenth-century, a legend was born out of the fearful rise of anti-Semitism. It went something like this...

Along the darkened, swampy banks of the Moldau River, just beyond Prague's city limits, the famous Rabbi Judah Loew ben Bezalel and his colleagues shaped a simple form in the near-frozen mud in that icy autumn of 1580. Anti-Jewish tensions and animosities were once more putting the city's Jewish community in grave danger. One night in a dream, the Rabbi received an answer to his constant prayers for help. That answer gave him details of a series of ancient rites, rites that convinced him to summon a protector from the lifeless riverbank mud.

They would create a golem.

The legends recall that the golem created from that mud was brought to life by the Rabbi, who carved special inscriptions into the creature's forehead. The golem — an animated anthropomorphic being — then set about protecting the Jews over a long period of time. However, after growing too powerful, the golem himself became uncontrollable. It began killing scores and scores of gentiles, seemingly at random. It also slayed some unfortunate members of the Jewish community. Despite the dangers it would bring onto the Jews by removing their protector, the Rabbi knew he had no choice but to undo the magic that had given the golem life.

Once it was done, the Rabbi confined the golem's now lifeless form to the attic of his synagogue. It remained sealed, and had apparently never been opened since.

John O'nians didn't believe in fairy tales. The legend of the Golem of Prague was just that, a fairy tale. It was a tale that, overall, had helped the Jewish people. That was, until it had gone wrong, when the golem's new power compelled it to start doing awful things. *Why is this crazy woman calling herself the new Golem?* To John that was confusing. And yet, O'nians sensed something sinister about her. The way she was so calm. The way she'd shot the woman in the head without flinching. That look in those piercing blue eyes...

John knew she was dangerous. She had already proven it.

A vicious slap to the cheek brutally interrupted his momentary recollection of the legend. He hadn't seen it coming, but it snapped him back to the present.

"Professor O'nians, Mr. Kane... it is time for the four of us to go on a little treasure hunt."

THE PRIZE

"WHAT IS IT EXACTLY YOU THINK I CAN FIND here?" Kane asked.

"Worry not, Mr. Kane. May I call you Hiram? I think we could be friends." That cold grin again. Those wild eyes.

Kane remained unmoved. Thinking.

Magda smiled. "I can tell you exactly what it is you will get for me, Mr. Kane. I think it should be worth the two million euros I need."

"What on earth do you need two million euros for? Are you just a greedy psychopath? Someone who'll get what she wants, with no regard for the lives of innocent women and children?" O'nians could not hide his contempt. Didn't want to.

"First of all, Professor, they are not innocent,"

said Magda. Her voice remained quiet, but there was malice in each syllable. "They are Jews. That means they are guilty. Their people have been corruptly ruling the world from behind their desks and banks, and from within governments, for centuries. Not centuries, thousands of years. They are swindling, lying pigs. So, no, they are not innocent, as you so naively put it. Not even close. Instead, they are criminals who deserve to be punished. However, as I have said on many occasions now, despite my better judgment, I will not hurt them. But, only if you deliver me what I need." Magda calmly lit a cigarette and took a couple of long, slow drags, never taking her eyes off the professor. She dropped the smoke to the floor and crushed it beneath her toe. Now she looked at Kane. "There is a network of tunnels beneath the city. They connect almost all the districts, both sides of the river, including beneath the castle and into the Lobkowicz Palace. You will go with me there, to the palace galleries. You will lead me to my reward. Your reward, in turn, will be the knowledge you have helped save nine lives. Nine worthless, Jewish lives." Magda spat on the floor, an unnerving combination of disgust and enjoyment on her face.

It was Kane's turn to protest. "That gallery will

be watched by armed security guards. I am no thief, and I have no idea how to steal anything, let alone priceless objects, without getting caught… maybe even shot and killed. I simply can't do it. I won't!"

Magda smiled again. She truly was enjoying herself. Then she turned, and without hesitation, she shot Professor O'nians in the arm. The smile never faltered.

The professor screamed in agony as blood began spilling from the wound and staining his yellow shirt. Kane launched himself towards Magda, but he was stopped short by another gunshot, the bullet exploding off the stone floor by his feet in an explosion of cement and razor-sharp tile fragments. He turned to see Marek Fitz pointing the gun at him. Kane knew that if he attacked the woman now it would all be over in seconds. Now they had both demonstrated their ability to fire at innocent people. He would not risk more lives.

John O'nians seethed, more out of anger than pain, though it was searing agony he felt. Luckily, the bullet had left more of a flesh wound than any significant damage. He was losing a lot of blood though, and it would need treating sooner rather than later.

"Can I tie a tourniquet around John's arm?" Kane asked.

Magda nodded. "Do not do anything stupid, Mr. Kane. You know what will happen if you do."

Kane returned the nod and rushed to John. He pulled off his blazer and ripped off a sleeve, quickly wrapping the makeshift bandage around John's forearm. "If you can, keep it raised. That should stem the flow of blood for a while." He looked his old friend in the eye. "You okay?"

"Yes, my boy, I'm fine. I have had worse, as you know." The two friends held each other's gaze. O'nians dare not ask Kane details of the plan he felt sure he had. They would be heard. It was too risky. "Let's do what they say," was all John said.

Kane and O'nians turned to face Magda and Marek. Kane said, "Lead the way."

RIDDLES

MAGDA SMILED AGAIN. "GOOD. IT IS THE SMART thing to do. The only thing. Now you will follow me."

It was after six in the evening. The autumn sun had long since disappeared over the western horizon. They didn't appear to be heading outside, so it mattered little. Kane knew, though, that at this time most museums and galleries around the city would be closed to the public. Any security would be reliant upon sensors and alarm systems, rather than beefed-up, gun-toting security guards. That was both good and bad. It meant he might not get shot trying to steal whatever it was this mad woman wanted stealing. However, he might end up in prison.

O'nians knew there were some impressive artefacts and artworks on display around Prague. He didn't know of any one piece in particular that might be worth as much as two million euros. It didn't really matter. If she believed that, whatever it was it was worth that much, and if it might help save the lives of those kids, then they would try their best to take it.

Magda led the way. Kane and O'nians followed. Marek Fitz walked close behind them, his gun constantly raised. As she approached a door in a back wall of the seminar hall, Magda paused and produced a key. She opened it and they filed through. She locked the door behind them. They were in some kind of store room. It was filled with nothing more than some stacked tables and chairs, and some dusty filing cabinets that looked as if no one had opened them in years, perhaps even decades. There didn't appear to be any other way out.

"What is this?" asked O'nians. Kane heard a slight tremor in his voice.

Magda glared at him for a moment. Then she stepped forward and pulled an old rug from the floor, revealing what looked like a hinged trap door. She leaned over and pulled it open. With a couple of deft manoeuvres, she had descended what the men soon realised were fold-out steps.

"Down, now!" barked Marek as he shoved the gun hard into Kane's back.

Kane's muscles tensed. He was more than ready to lash out and unleash fury at the motherfucker with the gun. Somehow he restrained himself. *Your time will come,* he thought as he edged towards the hole behind O'nians. John had taken a few steps down into the gloom.

Magda flicked a switch, and a bright lamp illuminated the dark passage. It was enough for them to see they were in a stone-hewn tunnel, which seemed to stretch out in both directions as far as they could see. Kane was surprised. He knew most ancient cities had tunnel networks dug deep beneath them. Their purpose was usually to help hated kings or despised emperors escape the wrath of their disgruntled or hungry subjects. Or to make hay with some rival or other's wife or daughter. Yet, Kane suspected these tunnels would have been sealed closed. Now they were being put to an equally clandestine use.

Magda smiled thoughtfully at O'nians. "That way," she said, pointing toward what O'nians believed was west.

"To the castle?" he asked.

"Very good, Professor. To the castle it is. Can you guess *where* in the castle, exactly?"

As John shuffled along the narrow passage, his arm throbbing in pain from the bullet injury, he thought about what might be of such interest at the castle. He knew of a couple of museums and a gallery. *What was it? The Lobkowicz? The palace?* "There's an old wealthy Czech family," he said. "The Lobkowicz? I believe they're the owners of the Lobkowicz Palace?"

"Correct again, Professor. Very well done. And, do you know what is in the palace gallery?"

Again, O'nians thought hard. He recalled seeing an article somewhere about some priceless musical instruments. The exhibit even included some original scores, and manuscripts, by composers such as Beethoven and Mozart, including Mozart's legendary 4th and 5th symphonies. *She wants us to steal music?* He wouldn't mention those, just in case she didn't know about them and added them to the list. "No. I don't. I have no idea what you're talking about."

"Really, Professor? I am a little surprised you cannot work it out. I thought it would be easy for a man of your obvious talents. You will find out soon enough. Now move."

For what seemed an age, they walked on along the twisting, undulating tunnel. Then the path started descending at a steeper gradient.

The river! Kane realised they must be passing deep beneath The Vltava. He silently marvelled at the skill of the ancient engineers to achieve such a truly incredible feat.

After a further twenty minutes they at last began to ascend. Another twenty minutes followed of negotiating the winding ups and downs of the tunnels. Finally, the passage opened up into a larger, cavern-like space.

"Stop here," Magda demanded. "Turn around and face that wall."

"Why do we need to —"

"Do what she fucking says," Marek snarled. His confidence was growing with every minute he held the gun. Like discovering his first hard on all over again.

Kane and O'nians did as they were told.

"Good.." Magda nodded. "You must understand, I cannot take any chances. I know Mr. Kane has a… shall we say, a special range of physical skills. I do not want to tempt him to use them."

"I am already tempted," Kane said quietly, glaring at the crazed woman.

"Let it remain no more than a temptation, then," she said back, smirking, as if to challenge him, to lure out the demons hidden within.

Kane's teeth ground together. His jowls twitched. He inhaled and said nothing. Did nothing. Yet.

A minute later both men had their hands bound tightly behind their backs. O'nians' arm was now agonising. The blood had almost stopped flowing, but the pain was getting serious.

"Now, listen carefully. Behind this door is another short tunnel. At the end of that tunnel is another door. That door leads directly into the Lobkowicz Palace. There will be no security guards operating at this time. There will of course be CCTV cameras in operation. A friend of mine has made sure the sensors to this door are disarmed. But, only this door. And, only for thirty minutes. That means that if you try to escape from any other exit, the alarms will sound. Then, I will lock you inside. If you do not acquire what I tell you to acquire, all within thirty minutes, again, I will lock you inside. They will catch you. They will not catch me. Nine people will die a slow and horrible death. Do you understand?"

Kane and O'nians shared another glance. Kane could tell the professor was struggling with the pain, though he was clearly fighting hard not to show it. Hiram himself was fighting a burning desire to smash out of his bonds, attack the bastards and put an end to the madness. He had fought tougher people than these and won. Although they had guns, Kane knew he could take them out given the chance. Yet, as long as the kids and their teacher were still held against their will, it was too risky. All the while the professor remained detained, his injury untreated, he simply could not take any chances. Not against such unhinged individuals.

Once more he stilled his racing heart and tried hard to calm down. "I understand," he finally said. John O'nians echoed the sentiment.

"Then, one minute from now I will open this door. You will go through it. The clock will start ticking the moment I close the door behind you. You will get me what I want. First, however, let us have a little fun. Professor, you are an art historian, are you not?"

O'nians nodded.

"And, do you not hail from East Anglia?"

"I do. So what?"

"So, you must be aware of a very well-known nineteenth-century painter whose most famous work was called —"

"The Hay Wain," finished Kane. "John Constable painted The Hay Wain."

"I am impressed, Mr. Kane. It seems you are not just a pretty face after all. Tough and handsome... always a winning combination. Sadly for you, it means we no longer need the good professor after all."

She turned and shot John O'nians.

FAILURE

"NO! WHAT THE FUCK ARE YOU DOING?" KANE yelled, apoplectic.

Magda simply grinned at him as O'nians slumped to the floor. "Thirty minutes, Mr. Kane. The clock is ticking."

Marek Fitz grabbed Kane by his arms before he could react. Magda slotted the large iron key into the ancient lock, and Kane looked on as it turned with a protesting screech.

"You have thirty minutes. Fail, and the professor, the teacher and the kids will die. Now go!"

With that, Marek's strong arms shoved Kane through the old door into darkness.

Kane stumbled into the darkness. He turned immediately and slammed his shoulder into the door. Then he did it again. And again. The heavy thuds echoed about the cavernous dark space.

It was futile. He had seen the look in the woman's eyes. There he recognised a look he had witnessed too often in the past. It was the look of someone who had moved beyond reason. Someone who had killed and would kill again. Someone beyond sanity.

Kane had come to believe that, even if he gave her the thing she wanted, it would not be enough to save the children. "Nor John," he whispered.

Yet, finding the object or artwork she wanted was his only chance of a positive outcome. At least if he found that and took it to her, he may have a chance of overpowering them and helping John. Then he would raise the alarm to the police about the missing children.

Kane turned. For a long moment, he stood still, allowing his eyes to adjust to the consuming darkness. After a few seconds, he could just begin to make out the vague shapes of walls, and doorways, and the glinting of some external light source reflecting off what must have been framed paintings. Kane's thoughts turned back to Constable and his painting, The Hay Wain. Kane knew that Constable's famous oil painting of the bucolic

Suffolk scene — Kane originated from Suffolk himself, and knew the area the painting was set in well, Flatford Mill on the River Stour — was definitely *not* on display in Prague. Instead, he knew it had hung In London's National Gallery for more than a century. *So, what does that have to do with whatever I'm supposed to be looking for? Is it even a painting? Something to do with agriculture?*

There was only one thing for it. Start looking for something related to that in some way, however tenuous it may seem.

Kane struggled against his bonds. Even if he found what he needed to find — unlikely in the darkness, and with only thirty minutes to do it in — he would need both hands free to claim it, whatever *it* was. Kane looked into the gloom and racked his brains. He hustled toward the greatest source of light he could find; a slanted orange arrow of light from what was probably a streetlamp outside the gallery. From there he paused again to let his eyes further adjust. Finally he saw something that gave him hope. It was a glass cabinet, housing a collection of exhibits.

Kane knew that if he smashed the glass and used a shard to cut his ties he would almost certainly set the alarms ringing. It was his only hope. If he were going to do that, he would have to wait until the last minute. First, he would locate his target. Then, he would race back to smash the glass and free his hands. Finally, he would have a matter of minutes, perhaps only seconds, to sprint back, snag the prize, and race back to the door and to the deranged woman awaiting him beyond. To the Golem of Prague. Unlike the myth, however, Kane knew for sure the woman truly was a monster. Anyone who could shoot dead an innocent woman, shoot an old man — twice — and potentially kill eight more children and their teacher, was clearly insane. Kane believed she was capable of anything.

He used that knowledge to inspire him. After a deep breath, Kane raced to the nearest cabinet, based on a hunch it was some kind of rare farming exhibit he was searching for. After several seconds' thought, however, he realised it couldn't have been that. W*hat farming artefact could possibly be worth that much money?*

He hustled into the next room. The light in there was a little better, due to more of the orange glow emanating from the outside. There he found more glass cabinets. These contained a vast range of ancient-looking musical instruments, which Kane suspected were actually very valuable. Looking closer in an adjacent case, he spotted something that surprised him: a series of open books, their pages displaying sheet music he guessed were original scores. Squinting hard, he read one of the placards:

Here you can see the original scores of Beethoven's 4th and 5th Symphonies, written between 1804 and 1806

Kane whistled. *Impressive,* he thought. Though they were certainly priceless, he felt sure they weren't what he was after.

He raced toward the next room of the palace gallery. When he realised it was a gallery almost entirely of paintings, he felt it must be the right place. Kane's art knowledge wasn't bad... studying under the great Professor O'nians saw to that. Painting wasn't his strong point. Yet, everyone from Suffolk knew of Constable's greatest work. He would have to scan every painting until he made the link.

There couldn't be long left now until his thirty minutes were over. *Probably ten more minutes*, he thought. He sprinted to the first wall, where he found portrait after portrait of one aristocrat or another. Kane's optimism waned a little. It wasn't until he entered the final room in the entire museum that he struck gold. He glanced up. Caught in one of the orange glowing beams of light was the item he was after. It was a large oil painting of a pastoral scene similar to that of Constable's The Hay Wain. He didn't recognise the image. Yet, when he looked at the identifying plaque he once more let out a low whistle. It said:

The Hay Harvest
Artist: Pieter Bruegel the Elder
Year: 1565
Type: Oil on wood

Pieter Brueghel the Elder, Kane knew, was a world-famous Flemish Renaissance painter. It meant the painting before him was worth an absolute fortune. *No wonder she wants this,* he mused. Remembering the ticking clock, he scanned the scene to see how he could actually take the painting. He was sure the frame itself was triggered with an alarm. After he shattered the glass the alarms would go off anyway, so that was nothing extra to worry about. Kane figured he would simply have to rip the entire frame off the wall. If the wood panel inside wouldn't easily lift out, he would take the whole thing with him. It was a shitty plan. It was the best he could come up with in the short time available.

His eyes were now well accustomed to the darkness. He sprinted back through the several doorways to the glass cases housing the Beethoven scores. After a deep breath, Kane shouldered through the surprisingly flimsy glass. It was no surprise, however, that the sudden shrieking of alarms pierced the silence. Kane carefully leant into the cabinet, and even more carefully, he positioned his wrists against an upright shard. Luckily, the cable-ties were brittle against such a sharp edge. Within thirty-seconds of measured efforts, first one, then the second and third ties pinged away. His hands were free.

Kane didn't wait to check for cuts. He didn't care if he had suffered any. Kane ran back to the Bruegel painting as the deafening alarms reminding him of the fearsome Nazgul from Lord of the Rings. *Why is it always Lord of the Rings characters?* he thought. *First Gollum, now the fucking Nazgul?* Despite his predicament, Kane's trademark wry grin crept for just a second onto his face. It was literally a second. This was no time for fun. Kane launched himself at the painting.

It did not budge. He tugged and tugged. It

would not yield. As the seconds ebbed away, so did his optimism. There was simply no way he could get the painting down.

His time was almost up. Hiram Kane knew he had failed.

The children, and his friend John O'nians, would die.

PRAYERS

JUDITH ANDERSON WAS DESPERATE.

She hadn't yet been able to free herself from her bonds. She felt half frozen to death. All she could think about was the poor kids.

Some of them had fallen asleep, thankfully. That was a blessing. She knew they must have been terrified, freezing and starving. They had been there almost four days now. Four days without food, and barely any water...

Is it four days? Five? Judith could no longer be sure. It was pitch black in the dungeons. She had long ago become disorientated and oblivious to what time it was. It was too long, that was for sure. Especially for the kids, who had, mercifully, amazed her with their stoicism and bravery. Judith knew that if she were one of them, she wouldn't be anywhere near as brave.

She only wished there was something more she could do to help them. Judith felt a sudden wave of failure settling over her. Hot tears came unbidden, and streamed down her cold cheeks.

Judith felt helpless. Desperate. Tormented by guilt and grief.

She slumped back against the bars of her cell and, for the first time in two decades, Judith prayed to a God she didn't believe in.

ROBBERY

PROFESSOR JOHN O'NIANS LAY UNMOVING.

He was unconscious, sprawled in a heap this side of the door they'd shoved Kane through. Dangerously weak from a loss of blood, now pooling like black oil around his prostrate form. At least he couldn't feel any pain.

Magda Pokorna cared nothing for the professor. She had used him only to lure Hiram Kane to help her. She had made up her mind to kill the professor the moment she'd learned he was going to be in Prague… extolling the virtues of the Jew pigs' art.

It was true she could have asked anyone to help her in her endeavours. Magda knew enough men who shared her hatred, men who would have got involved in this kind of thing for the right reward.

Many of them would do anything for sex with her... many had proved it often. She had discarded all of them. Some of them she'd killed.

She had learned of Kane from reading about his exploits in the papers over the last couple of years. She knew he was both handsome and courageous. He was also wealthy. Magda wanted him sexually. She would make sure she had him before she killed him.

Her priority was always the Bruegel painting. She knew it was worth millions; way more than the two million she had told the men earlier. Some so-called art experts believe it would fetch as much as ten million in today's inflated market. It was more than enough for what she needed.

Magda couldn't help herself. She wanted some fun, too. She was already having fun with Hiram Kane.

HE KNEW HE HAD FAILED. Unless…

Kane sprinted back to the previous room, where, from the corner of his eye, he'd spotted a rack mounted on a wall that held a collection of ancient swords. When he got there, he paused. The last time he'd seen a sword like this he had witnessed it, at close hand, slicing off the head of a Yakuza gangster. It had been a gruesome sight he would never forget. Again, he had no time to dwell.

He snatched down one of the weighty swords. It looked to be an ancient Crusader-era weapon, the kind a Templar Knight might have used to fight the Saracens. It had been blunted for obvious reasons. And cleaned. There remained no evidence of the deaths it had caused. It would serve his purpose. Kane ran back to the Bruegel.

After a few deep breaths, using his considerable strength Kane wedged the sword into the crack between the wall and the painting. Using it like a crow bar, he pushed.

It worked. The huge, heavy frame creaked away from the wall a few centimetres. He eased the sword in a little further. A moment later he shuffled to the other side and did the same, sliding the sword up and in, inch by inch. Eventually something gave way, and the entire frame — and the priceless painting by Pieter Bruegel the Elder within — crashed to the floor. It sounded so loud in the otherwise silent gallery. It was immediately superseded by the deafening alarms.

Kane reached down and hauled up the frame.

He knew he had only a minute or two more before being locked inside the palace museum. So, he ran.

Twenty-seconds later he stood panting outside the original door. He was about to knock, then paused. A thought came to him. He didn't trust the woman... the Golem. Not one bit. She would not let them go after he'd given her the painting. Neither did he trust that she would tell them the location of the kids. Hiram at least needed to remove Marek Fitz from the equation. He didn't believe the man was a natural killer. He did have a gun, and if pushed into a corner, pressured by the woman, he would probably use it. Kane was no killer either... *Just have to take him down in my own special way*, he mused. He would relish the moment. Kane glanced up.

Surrounding the door was an ornate, decorative stone frame, almost like two pilasters supporting a huge lintel. It was so deep in fact, it formed a ledge above the door. Kane believed that if he could climb above the door, and wait — he was banking on the fact Magda would send Marek out to check — then he could jump down, incapacitate Marek, and lock him inside the gallery room before anyone could react. If the prick lost a fucking hand in the process, so be it. The bastard would think twice about using his other one to point guns at innocent people.

Kane hoped he might even get the chance to take out Magda, too. He suspected she was too smart to be tricked that easily. There was also John to consider.

Kane placed the framed painting against the wall, behind the impressive pilaster and out of sight for when the door opened. Next he lifted over a nearby chair. Then he reached up, grabbed the sturdy stone frame, and deftly swung himself up and onto the lintel. Once set, he stole a deep breath. It was a good idea. It might even work. He positioned the sword as such that he could leap down with it. Another long inhale. Seconds were ticking.

He leant over and knocked hard on the door.

He only had to wait three seconds. The old key turned in the lock. Kane held his breath. Two more seconds. Then, just as he suspected, Marek stepped slowly through the doorway. His arm outstretched, the gun held aloft. Kane didn't wait to see his reaction. Kane dropped to the ground, the sword raised in both hands. As his feet struck the wooden floor together, so the raised sword struck down onto Marek's arm. It connected just above the wrist, severing everything by the sheer force of the blow rather than because it was sharp. The gun, and Marek's hand, thunked to the floor. The gun clattered away out of reach.

Kane held his balance. Without waiting to see what happened, he snatched up the painting with his free hand and darted through the door. He slammed it shut behind him.

To his surprise, such was his speed of his actions, he had caught Magda off-guard. He almost had time to impale her with the sword. Of course, he wouldn't do that. He hesitated a fraction of a second as he assessed the options. At the vital moment, however, Magda understood what was happening. She levelled the gun at Professor O'nians' head.

"Do you want me to shoot him again, Mr. Kane?"

Kane stopped sharp. He was a split second too slow. He placed the Bruegel down. He kept hold of the sword a second too long. Magda fired, missing O'nians' leg by an inch. Kane wasn't sure if that was deliberate or not. It was inspiration enough for him to put down the ancient weapon.

"Very resourceful, Mr. Kane, as I knew you would be. And the Brueghel... isn't it beautiful?"

"I did what you asked. Where are the children? Tell me where they are. Let them go."

"Oh, Mr. Kane, so demanding. It's sexy. But I am not finished with you yet. Move away from the sword." She nodded toward the first door they had arrived through. Kane did as she told him.

"Good. I still have one more task for you. For that task, however, we need to go somewhere else. Our work here is done. Except one more teeny, tiny little detail." Magda Pokorna smiled that cruel, maniacal smile.

She turned and pointed the gun once more at O'nians' prone figure.

And fired.

BECOMING

"NOOO!" KANE BELLOWED. "WHAT THE FUCK… what… have you done?!"

Magda turned back to Kane. "He is an old man who has served his purpose today. He has proved his Jewish sympathies. He deserved it. Anyway, I only needed him to get to you. It was always about you, Mr. Kane... and my special prize, of course."

Magda eyed Hiram Kane with those piercing blue eyes, eyes that had lured dozens of weak men to her bed. Many never lived to tell the tale. To Magda they were just toys, pastimes that empowered her to become what she wanted to become. She knew she was a powerful, independent woman who got whatever — or whoever — she wanted, whenever she wanted it. Those victims, her victories, had helped her become the Golem of Prague.

She inwardly admitted she was probably a little crazy. Insane, even. The authorities knew it too. It's why she had changed her identity multiple times over the last two decades. It was necessary. She had served time in prison for brutally murdering her own mother. Magda thought that prison time was worth it. She actually enjoyed some of it. They'd classified her as a minor then, yet in prison she didn't behave like one. Yet, they released her after serving just a few years of her sentence. She still didn't know why. She didn't care.

Magda's mother was a sinner. She had always known her mother deserved to die. Magda's mother was Jewish.

Her father, however, was not a Jew. Over the years during Magda's childhood he had developed into a hard-core anti-Semite. Nevertheless, he loved his wife, and never laid a finger on her — despite the way she treated him, the way she taunted him. Instead, he saved his aggression for someone else. His daughter.

Magda never blamed her father for the harsh beatings. Never. She knew the truth. He was innocent. If he were guilty of anything, it was of being such a fucking pussy. It was her Jew pig mother that had caused it all. As soon as Magda was capable — after her father finally left his wife after years of misery and shame — Magda killed her. It was a gruesome death.

She sedated her mother with animal tranquil-lisers she'd acquired from a friend. When her mother had passed out, Magda tied her up and doused her and the bedroom with petrol. With a can of yellow spray paint, she had painted the Star of David on the bed. Then she laid her mother's body out, aligning her hands, feet and head with five points of the star. It was a crude representation. She smiled as she did it.

Magda calmly smoked a cigarette, whistling between drags. When it was halfway burned down, she dropped it onto the bed. She watched impas-sively as the sheets slowly engulfed her mother in a deadly, flaming holocaust. As her mother began to stir, Magda smiled, turned and walked down the stairs. She left the apartment for the very last time.

Fifteen-year-old Magda Pokorna never looked back.

The authorities soon discovered her mother's charred remains. Magda was later found and arrested; a neighbour spotted her leaving the apartment at the time of the blaze. She did not resist, and calmly admitted her actions. She never shed a single tear about it.

Since that heart-warming moment of growth, Magda had, at last count, killed twenty-four Jews. By the end of this day, she knew that number of dead Jews would rise to thirty three. Thirty five, if she counted the professor and Hiram Kane. Sadly they weren't Jews. Oh well…

But, she wouldn't kill Kane yet, at least not until she'd had her fun with the handsome Englishman.

KANE WAS IN SHOCK. He hustled over to his friend. He expected to find the old man dead. Unbelievably, the professor was still breathing, though his breaths came as laboured, almost imperceptible gasps. Kane was torn. If he tried convincing Magda John was alive and needed a hospital, he knew she would just shoot him again. Probably himself, too. If Kane made out John was dead, and they left him there, he would probably die of his wounds within minutes.

Thinking fast, he took his chances on the latter. Kane stood up and turned to face the psycho. He glared at her. His hands squeezed into powerful white-knuckled fists. Through clenched teeth, he said, "You have killed him. He's dead. My friend is dead. I will… I will do as you ask."

"That's good, Mr. Kane. I can see how angry you are. It is... it is sexy. I do like my men angry and powerful." She nodded toward the door. "Open it. It is time for some fun."

THE CHALLENGE

JUDITH ANDERSON AWOKE FROM HER SLUMBER.

She'd been having a nightmare about some kids — her students? They were chained up like animals in a dungeon. Yet it was so real. She stretched. At least, she tried to stretch. She realised she too was chained up. That's when the shocking truth came back to her in a sickening moment of heart-breaking reality.

The sudden, distant creaking of what sounded like an ancient door set her heart hammering in her chest.

Some of the kids had woken too. She called out to them. "It is okay, children," she lied. "I am here. Everything will be okay," she said again. She knew it would not be.

She strained her ears to listen over the rising murmur of fear among the kids. Now she couldn't hear anything along the pitch-dark tunnel. The kids were growing hysterical. Fear and thirst and hunger were finally taking their toll on the youngsters.

Then Judith spotted a flickering beam of light. It looked like a torch beam bouncing off the walls. It was getting closer. She forced her tired, swollen eyes wide, trying to absorb as much light as possible in an effort to see who was approaching. With growing horror she knew it was the crazy woman who had kidnapped her and the kids. The woman who had locked them down there like lepers.

To her surprise, when the light was sufficient the first person she saw was not the blonde-haired woman. Instead it was a tall man she'd never seen before. *Has he come to rescue us?*

Judith felt a wave of hope. That fleeting glimmer of hope was instantly dashed when she spotted the woman behind the man. Worse, she held a gun against his back.

The kids had fallen silent. They too had seen the gun, its silver barrel glinting under the torch beam. Suddenly, the woman reached behind her and flicked a switch. It bathed the whole tunnel and dungeon system in a blinding white light. It hurt their eyes after being sprawled in blackness for so many days.

Kane's heart sank when he saw the state of the woman and the children. They looked scared, dirty and hungry. All bar none of their puffy cheeks were stained with tears.

"What have you done?" Kane said to Magda, his voice low. "They're just children. They've done nothing to you."

"You're right. They've done nothing *to* me, except assaulted me with their foul Jewishness. But they have done something *for* me. They convinced you to help me. For that I am grateful. In due course I will reward them for their service. First, a test. It is a test I think you will pass."

"Me? What're you talking about?"

"Mr. Kane, of all people, you know how guilt can serve as a powerful emotion. At least, that is what I have come to believe. I myself feel no guilt. Not a drop. I have a purpose to my actions. I do them without pause or regret. Quite often with pleasure. Some people simply do not deserve to live." Magda paused, and waved the gun toward the frightened children. "For example, what you see here are children. You are wrong. They are animals.

Jewish animals. Their parents are Jewish. If I let them live, their spawn will be Jewish. It is my responsibility to stop that from happening. I would happily kill them all."

"You're insane. You are fucking insane!"

Magda just smiled. "That is probably partly true. I have indeed been labelled insane before. However, I am not irrational. I am merely fulfilling my duties for the greater good. Anyway, back to the test. I am going to set you a series of challenges. For each challenge you pass, one of these pigs will escape slaughter. I will allow it to go free. It is a simple challenge, Mr. Kane. I feel sure that, because of all that precious guilt you hold close, like a noose around your neck, it is a challenge in which you will succeed. After all, I believe you know and understand the consequences of failure."

If it were possible, the smile on the woman's face grew even wider than before. Even more cruel. She was enjoying herself. Kane knew without doubt she was unhinged and would carry out her threat to kill the children in a heartbeat. It was likely she would do that anyway, even if he complied with the challenge. Whatever the hell the challenge was. It was his only hope. "What must I do?"

"It is very simple. The Star of David has six

points. That woman... the Woman of Judea," spat Magda. "She has two hands, two feet and an ugly head. She probably has a tail too." Magda smirked. "You also have those same extremities, though since you are not Jewish, I do not believe you have a tail, unlike these rats. Anyway, your first challenge is to choose one of her extremities. Then you will fire a bullet through it. If you do that, I will let one of the rats go free."

"You cannot expect me to shoot an innocent —"

"No, I can not expect that," she cut in. "You will do it anyway. You know what will happen if you do not. Let me make it easy on you. I will choose. First, you will shoot her through one of her thieving Jew hands. Then you will do it again with the other. Then, you will shoot each of her scurrying feet. And for the fifth bullet... Well, you get the idea." Magda reached into her waistband and pulled out another pistol, this one smaller than her own. "I am going to hand this to you. I am not stupid."

She approached the child at the end of the line — the fearless tubby kid who first led his friends into the tunnel. She deftly undid the padlock linking him to the others. She dragged him upright, though his legs buckled from exhaustion. Magda hauled him to his feet. Kane saw the fear in the boy's eyes, yet he did not cry out. He seemed to understand what was going on.

Brave kid, Kane thought. His rage grew by the second.

Magda thrust the boy in front of her, then pushed the barrel of her gun against the back of his head. The other kids wailed, stricken with fear. Still the kid kept his control. Judith too was crying, not from fear of what the woman was making the man do to her, but for the children. Her students. She would happily sacrifice herself for their lives.

Magda tossed the gun onto the floor. She motioned for Kane to pick it up. "I'm sure you know how to use that. You also know what you must do with it."

Kane stood motionless, frozen to the spot for a long moment. He found himself unable to move, horrified about what she was demanding of him. His breaths were deep, quick and raspy, almost as if he was on the verge of a panic attack. He looked at the woman, the kids' teacher, their eyes locking for long seconds. Kane sensed in those eyes she was giving him permission to save the children at any costs. He fought back the rising bile. She wanted him to shoot her to save the kids. He turned to

Magda. Saw her maniacal blue eyes glaring at him. Then turned to face the kids.

I cannot let them die.

I *will* not let them die.

Kane turned back to face the teacher.

"My name's Judith," she said. "Please, do as she asks."

"I... I can't," Kane muttered. "I can't do it." He turned to Magda. "I will shoot myself right now. Just let the kids go. They're just children. They've done nothing to you."

"Mr. Kane, I admire your courage. But, I am making the rules here. You will do as I say." Magda nodded at Judith, who was staring intently at Hiram Kane. "You will do it now."

"Just do it," Judith said, her eyes unwavering from Kane's. She held her hands above her head, giving him his target. "Just do it... do it now!" she screamed, pleading. Desperate.

Kane raised the gun.

It shook slightly. He felt the resistance of the trigger beneath his finger. Kane's nerves were wracked from stress and guilt and fear, and of the grief to come. He hesitated and hesitated, and…

Then he took aim, closed his eyes.

And squeezed.

CHAOS

MAGDA WATCHED ON WITH INTENSE GLEE AS Kane's emotions threatened to break him.

She grinned as the bitch rat named Judith shouted at him, encouraging him to fire. Magda chuckled. She knew that, no matter what happened, she would be the only one to depart this tunnel alive. She would leave in her wake a beautiful pile of Jewish corpses, topped by a dead Englishman.

"Do it now!" screamed Judith.

Kane fired.

Right at that moment, the kid in front of Magda leant forward. At the exact second Kane pulled the trigger, he slammed his head back into Magda Pokorna's face. It caught her by surprise and smashed her nose. Blood exploded everywhere. Her gun toppled to the floor. The other kids screamed as Judith collapsed to the stony ground.

Kane had missed. Whether he meant it or not, the bullet had slammed into the brittle stone on the wall surrounding the iron cleat that held Judith prisoner, just as she ducked as he'd fired. There stone crumbled and the cleat fell free. It took Judith only a second to realise she was free. She staggered to her feet.

Chaos ensued. The brave kid had turned, and scrambled to reach the gun before Magda. He was too slow. She screamed as she grabbed it and pointed it at his face. Her finger slipped on the trigger, now smeared with her own blood, and she misfired. She half grinned, half snarled beneath her battered, bloodied nose. This time her grip was true. She fired at the kid. The range was point blank.

Yet Judith was faster. A split second before Magda pulled the trigger she launched herself through the air in front of the boy. The bullet slammed into her chest. She crumpled to the floor in a heap as Magda screamed in frustrated rage.

Magda recovered immediately. She was about to fire again when her hand exploded in a mass of blood and bone and obliterated fingers. A bullet from the first gun Hiram Kane had ever fired destroyed her right hand forever.

The cacophony of chaos fell to a few muted whimpers, emanating from the terrified children. Kane rushed over to Magda. Within a few seconds he had restrained her with extra chains discarded on the floor. A quick search of her pockets revealed a set of keys. Kane assumed most were for the padlocks securing the kids. Next he rushed to the boy. He was shaking, but otherwise fine. Judith had saved his life.

"Just a moment kids," he said quietly, unsure if they understood. "It is almost over."

Judith remained unmoved. Kane gently rolled her over. He immediately feared the worst. A growing circle of blood had drenched the front of her jumper and was beginning to seep onto the stone floor. She was breathing, but they were slow, shallow breaths. Kane swallowed hard. He knew they would be among her last. He turned to the brave boy, who stood there now, looking on with wide-eyed concern.

"Do you speak English," Kane asked.

"Yes. Miss Anderson was... is... our English teacher."

"Okay, good. What's your name?"

"Tomáš."

"Very good, Tomáš. You are a very brave young man. I need you to be brave for just a little longer. Can you do that?"

Tomáš nodded. "Okay." He smiled. It was forced.

"Tomáš, I'm going to take Miss Anderson out of here and to a hospital. I have to go now. Can you stay and unlock your friends?" Tomáš nodded. "Here are the keys. Can you do that for me? Can you stay here and help the others?" He tossed the keys to Tomáš, who deftly caught them. He nodded again, stoic.

"That's very good, Tomáš. When you're all free of those chains, follow out the way I go, okay? Try and find someone to take you to hospital. I will call the police as soon as I am outside."

Tomáš took a couple of deep breaths. Despite the cold of the tunnel, the kid was sweating. Kane had never known a braver kid in his life.

"I will do it," Tomáš said.

Kane nodded. His thoughts briefly turned to John O'nians. Kane knew that by taking Judith instead of returning for his friend, he was lessening any hope of the professor surviving his injuries. The amount of blood he'd lost was critical, Kane was sure. Yet, he was just as sure that if John had known what had happened here in the tunnel, he would absolutely want his friend to focus on saving the woman and the kids.

Good luck, John, old friend, thought Kane. With that, he carefully hoisted Judith Anderson over his powerful shoulders. With an encouraging nod to Tomáš, he hustled the teacher's inert form along the dark corridor.

In his heart of hearts, he knew it was already too late.

DEATH & LIFE

AN HOUR LATER.

Hiram Kane sat alone in the waiting room at the nearby Hospital Na Františku.

He had managed to carry Judith out of the tunnels and onto the castle's main plaza. A swarm of police stood hassling journalists, gathered there after the alarms of the Lobkowicz Palace gallery had been set off. Kane's concern was that he'd be arrested and taken down, maybe even shot. Somehow, though, he had convinced the police he was innocent and was doing a good public service and taking the victim to the hospital. He learned later that Marek Fitz, the journalist, had broken down in tears after his arrest. He had told the police everything. Almost. He neglected the part about Kane chopping his hand off. His conscience had gotten the better of him, and he told the police Hiram Kane was innocent. *The mad woman was right,* Kane mused. *Guilt is a powerful emotion.*

A minute after that Kane and Judith were being driven fast along Thunovská Road towards the hospital in a police car. On route he told the police the location of the children, John O'nians, and of course, Magda Pokorna. The police officer radioed a colleague. He told Kane that an armed unit was already on its way, as well as a team of first responder medics.

Despite the evidence of what he'd seen, Kane held out a slim glimmer of hope that his friend John O'nians was somehow still alive. It was just a glimmer. With all the blood John had lost, surviving the ordeal was unlikely, despite the old man's stubborn resilience. It was a toughness Kane had witnessed on numerous occasions over the years. Kane hoped there was still a little of that fire burning in John's belly.

There was some good news. All eight children that had been kidnapped and held captive by Magda Pokorna were alive and doing well. They were malnourished and dangerously dehydrated. Yet, aside from than the mental scars they'd surely suffer, the hospital staff assured Kane they would all make a full physical recovery.

The thud of a gently closing door roused Kane from his melancholy. He glanced up, and saw the surgeon he'd spoken to earlier approaching from down the corridor. Kane swallowed. The grave look on the surgeon's face confirmed to Kane everything he already feared. The surgeon paused at Kane's side and placed a hand on his shoulder.

"I am very sorry, Mr. Kane. She was deceased before you arrived. There was nothing more you could have done."

Kane inhaled, then slowly exhaled. It wasn't a surprise. But the blow was bitter. He stood up and shook the man's hand. "Thank you for your efforts, Doctor," was all he said.

Hiram Kane turned and walked along the corridor, knowing, in his heart of hearts, there was always more that could be done.

Always.

DESPAIR

KANE HAD NEVER BEEN A MAN WHO BELIEVED IN miracles.

And yet, he somehow wasn't surprised when he learned that, by what indeed must have been some kind of physical miracle — he definitely didn't believe in the spiritual kind — John O'nians had survived.

Not only had he survived, but he was now sitting up and chatting amiably to a rather attractive nurse called Elizabeth. When John saw his old friend approaching, both men smiled widely. In truth, Kane's smile was more a smile of bewildered astonishment than happiness.

"But how? I... I saw you on the floor. I thought... there was no chance you could have —"

"— survived?" O'nians finished. "You should know by now, Hiram, not everything is as it seems. Yes, she shot me. It wasn't that bad of an injury. I knew it likely wouldn't prove to be a lethal wound. I also knew that if I played dead she might not shoot me again. I trusted my instincts that you wouldn't do something stupid and get yourself killed."

Kane shook his head and sighed. "You always were a tough old bastard." Kane recalled once again those many times back in his university seminar rooms, when John would seemingly be asleep. It was an uncanny gift that had undone many a student at many universities across the world. This iteration was a new twist. John had reconstituted it to save his own life.

"I guess I should've known better," Kane said, and leaned in and gave his old friend and mentor a warm hug. "I'll leave you to the nurse." He smiled and headed for the door. O'nians winked and smiled back.

Kane left the private ward and trudged down the corridor, his smile slipping away with every step. He made his way out of the hospital and stepped out into the cool night air of beautiful Prague.

Kane was devastated. Another person — this

time an innocent teacher, Judith Anderson — had died because of him.

When will it ever stop? he thought. *When will it ever stop?*

As a chilly rain began to fall gently from above that ancient, troubled city, so rare tears of despair fell from Hiram Kane's eyes.

EPILOGUE

THAT'S JUST THE WAY SHIT ROLLED FOR HIRAM KANE.

KANE'S TRIP to Prague to visit his old friend Professor John O'nians had somehow descended from a peaceful seminar into a deadly conflict. *Why does this always happen to me?* he mused. Yet, Hiram Kane was far from amused.

In fact, he was thoroughly pissed off. He stayed in the city a while, monitoring John's recovery from his injuries and visiting all the kids he'd help save. He had been asked to provide testimony to detectives of the Prague Police, who, over several meetings, had pieced together the bizarre events that took place above and below Prague.

Now that he'd had a few days to reflect on it all,

Kane realised that no matter where he went or what he did, and no matter how low of a profile he tried to keep, trouble always came knocking at his door. And he fucking was sick of it.

Kane gazed across at the famous, ancient clock tower in Prague's Old Town Square as he finished off the latest of several Czech beers. Then ordered another one. He glanced across the table and smiled.

"You'd miss it if you stopped," the woman said. She winked, in the way only Alexandria Ridley could wink. After hearing about Kane's latest plight, the long-term love of his life, the beautiful art historian, Alex Ridley, had flown out to Prague on the next available flight.

"No I wouldn't," he said. "This time I've had enough."

Alex noticed the usual glint in his eye, just above the trademark wry smile. She sensed this time he might actually mean it. It would be the first time ever.

"However," Kane continued, "I think it might just be time to return to the homeland for a bit, catch up with some old friends. I fancy laying low at the estate for a few months. After seeing that Bruegel painting, and thinking about Constable country, it got me yearning for my childhood haunts. I'm going to help John travel home first, once he's fit enough. Knowing him it will be hours rather than days. I figured I might stick around in Suffolk for a while before heading back to Cuzco. Fancy joining me?"

"I do," Alex said. "Someone's got to keep you out of trouble."

Kane smiled. He almost chuckled. It was Suffolk. Not even Hiram Kane could find trouble in sleepy Suffolk.

But Hiram Kane had been wrong before.

THE END

LIKE THAT? THEN YOU'LL LOVE THESE!

Book 0 — The Golem of Prague

Book 1 — The Tiger Temple

Book 2 — The Samurai Code

Book 3 — The Condor Prophecy

Book 4 — The Shadow of Kailash

Book 5 — The Feathered Serpent

Book 6 — Of Curses and Kings

Book 7 — Silent Knight: Origin Story

Book 8 — The Oak Island Enigma

The Hiram Kane Box Set #I

The Hiram Kane Box Set #2

The Alexandria Ridley Vigilante Thrillers

Book 0 - I, Survivor

Book 1 — I, Vigilante

Book 2 — I, Guardian

Book 3 — I, Salvation

COLLABORATIONS

The Liberator Thrillers with Luke Richardson

Set Him Free

Set You Free

Set Them Free

Set Me Free

Apocalyptic Thrillers with Jay Tinsiano

ARK: Outbreak

Vigilante Media Thrillers with Edie Kaufman

Day of the Dead

Literary Fiction by me, Steven Moore

I Have Lived Today: A Boy's Coming of Age Story

THE TIGER TEMPLE: AN EXCERPT

INCENSE HUNG THICK IN THE AIR, ITS BLUISH-GREY haze adding to the somewhat mystical atmosphere. In the temple's inner sanctum, the organic frangipani scent synonymous with religious ceremonies in the village of Nyuh Kuning permeated every corner.

From somewhere out of sight, the haunting melodic chimes of the *rindik* musicians added a second layer of mystique. Coupled with the unique architecture, and shrine after shrine laden with flowers and offerings, Hiram Kane was again reminded that Bali truly was the 'Island of the Gods'.

Standing beside Hiram were Ketut and Putu, two brothers who had become his close friends since he'd arrived in their village almost three months previous. Ketut was lean, clean cut and good looking, and a popular resident of the community of eight-hundred that called Nyuh Kuning home. His shaggy hair gave him the appearance of a twenty-eight-year-old teenager, and Kane teased him for being the long-lost fifth member of The Beatles.

Putu was the older brother at thirty-seven. He was taller and broad shouldered, and handsome in a rugged way, but with watchful eyes and an air of menace about him he was acutely aware of and that had served him well in his younger years. The shaved head and huge tattooed biceps enhanced the look. And yet, despite his tough appearance Putu was lively, quick with a smile, and the type of man who would do anything for anyone. Sadly, that was often to his own detriment.

The physical difference between the siblings was stark, and Ketut's flip-flops were no match for Putu's heavy biker boots. But the love between the brothers was there for all to see. Their mutual respect was genuine and inspiring to Hiram, who, since he'd got to know them better over the last few months, had come to trust the brothers as if they were his own kin.

The colourful ceremony at the *pura puseh*, the

'Temple of Origin' located in the east of the village, thus nearer to the spiritually important Mount Agung volcano, was to honour the Balinese Hindu God *Betara Desa*. The annual event was a social highlight of the community, when the men got together to complain about taxes, the cost of scooter fuel and their aching joints, and the women got together to complain about the men. There was, of course, a lot of praying.

Hiram wasn't a religious man, but he'd always been fascinated by religion, a dissonance he was comfortable with. It gave him a chance to witness beautiful art and architecture, and visit peaceful, atmospheric ceremonies and temples such as this.

The three men stood to the rear of the temple. The brothers focused on the words of the priest, while Hiram watched with fascination as everyone present paid their respects to Betara Desa. Even the effervescent children were still and quiet, their attention where it was supposed to be. Hiram felt a deep respect for the serene and innate discipline so evident in Balinese people.

Gazing through the swirling incense clouds and the throng of bodies, he caught a glimpse of a young girl, who happened to turn and catch his eye. Her mischievous smile would have melted any heart, and Hiram had a momentary pang of regret he'd decided not to have kids of his own. But as always, it was gone in a flash. Hiram knew that the adventurous, spontaneous lifestyle he enjoyed and the scrapes he all too often found himself in, plus the dangerous overpopulating of the planet, meant not having kids was one of the few sensible decisions he'd ever made. Besides, he'd yet to convince the long-term yet unrequited love of his life, the beautiful art historian Alexandria Ridley, to even commit to a relationship. So no, Hiram loved kids, but he would leave producing them to other people.

He recognised the pretty little girl in the jade green dress… Ayu? She turned away, but before she did she poked her tongue out at him. He promptly returned the compliment. Before she disappeared back into the crowd the last thing Hiram saw was the stuffed toy tiger that had seemed permanently attached to her hand since he'd first seen her around the village.

Crack. Crack. Crack.

The unmistakable retort of gunshots echoed around the temple, but an instant later the place had fallen silent as the worshippers processed the shocking sounds.

A moment later the place erupted in a chaotic

chorus of screams and shouts and a crush of bodies as the terrified villagers scrambled towards the exit. Before he could react Hiram felt himself forced back against the inner wall, unable to resist the manic surge of bodies and the flailing arms of the fear-stricken worshippers. Forced back into the same corner, Ketut locked eyes with his friend. Shock and fear were written on his face, his wild eyes telling their own story.

The screaming and surging continued as close to three-hundred people hustled to safety, the unknown gunman still elusive.

"What the hell's going on?" Hiram shouted to Ketut, who remained speechless. "Are you hurt?"

Ketut shook his head, his mouth agape.

"Ketut? Are you injured?" he pressed.

"No… no. I am okay. Where… Where is Putu?"

Hiram glanced among the hordes, finally thinning as the majority of temple goers had at last made it outside.

"I can't see him," Hiram yelled above the still rowdy bedlam. "Let's get out of here."

They joined the last stream of villagers, acutely aware there may still be a gunman in the temple, when Hiram's ears pricked up at the most pitiful wailing he'd ever heard. It was a woman, crying out for… for Ayu?

"Where is my daughter? Where is Ayu?" she howled in her native Balinese. Recognising that final word, Hiram was instantly on high alert. He glanced at Ketut, who had also heard those dreadful cries. With horror Hiram remembered Ayu was Ketut's niece.

With single-minded determination Ketut forced his way through the crowds and burst outside, the sudden bright sunlight momentarily blinding him.

Hiram joined him seconds later, and a moment after that Putu arrived. The man was panic-stricken.

"Where is Ayu?" he bellowed. "Where is my niece?"

Just then the ascending growl of powerful motorbike engines thundered above the hum of the crowd. Hiram swivelled upon hearing that roaring chaos, turning in time to witness a scene he would never forget; little Ayu being shoved roughly onto a motorbike seat and clamped between the legs of a man. After catching Hiram's eye and holding that glare for a few seconds, the big man pulled down his blacked-out visor and accelerated away from the temple, two other huge bikes right on his tail and scattering bewildered worshippers in all directions.

Without a second's hesitation Hiram grabbed the brothers. "With me. Now!"

Neither Ketut nor Putu had seen what their friend had witnessed, but they knew him well enough by now not to doubt him. As he sprinted off to the rear of the temple towards their own motor-bikes, they followed. Less than fifteen seconds later the trio were tearing up the main road through Nyuh Kuning towards the sacred Monkey Forest, on what had suddenly turned into a rescue mission.

Like this? Buy it NOW:

The Tiger Temple

YOUR REVIEW CAN MAKE A HUGE DIFFERENCE

Reviews are so helpful to an author. They give us the platform and the confidence to continue doing what we love. As an independently published author, I don't have the luxury of being backed by a big publishing house. Instead, I have to rely on the quality of my writing, the ability of my stories to move people, and the generosity of my readers.

More importantly, however, reviews serve you, the reader, and readers like you. They help inform a potential reader if they're buying a book they will like, so they can spend their hard-earned money with more confidence.

Thus, if you leave an honest review, everyone's a winner.

If you enjoyed ***The Golem of Prague*** I'd be

very grateful if you could spend just a couple of minutes leaving an honest review on the book's Amazon page. You can access that easily by clicking below:

Please review The Golem of Prague now!

Thank you very much,

Steven

AUTHOR'S NOTE

HELLO THERE. STEVEN MOORE, HERE.

Thanks so much for reading ***The Golem of Prague.*** I hope you enjoyed it.

I often get asked where my story ideas emanate. The simple answer? From my extensive travels around the world and the wonderful experiences they've given me.

I first left my home country of England aged nineteen, and I've been travelling ever since — that's nearly three decades (sshhh…). I've been fortunate enough to have visited some incredible places, and have met the most inspiring people. Combine that with real world events, historical characters, exotic locations, current social issues, my own interests and passions, and a large slice of imagination, and I have some pretty motivating material.

How about my protagonist, Hiram Kane? Well, insiders might say I'm writing about myself. Kane has an archaeology and art history degree, as do I. Just like Kane, I didn't follow through with my Masters' studies. Instead I chose a different path, like Kane. I have been on many similar adventures to our protagonist, and I have visited or lived in all the countries that feature in the Hiram Kane action thriller series, from Peru to Egypt, to India, and beyond. Also, like Hiram, I've found myself in more than a few dicey situations and it could be argued that I've been lucky to have come through a few of them.

I actually live in San Miguel de Allende, Mexico, with my writer wife and our two rescue cats, Ernest Hemingway & F Scott Fitzgerald (Ernie and Fitz). Thus, inspiration for exciting action and adventure in mysterious, enigmatic settings, is never, ever far away.

Once again, thanks for reading myself story. I hope you're intrigued to check out the rest of the series.

Would you like to sign up for my bi-weekly, spam-free newsletter?

Sound good? Then simply click this link:

SIGN ME UP

ACKNOWLEDGMENTS

I don't know any author who can finish a book of any kind without a lot of help and support. I'm certainly no different. The assistance I received for this story, and for all the books in the Hiram Kane series, has been both necessary and invaluable.

In this case, however, I'm reserving my written thanks to my good friends, Mark Fitzhenry & Magda Pokorna. Mark was a footy (soccer) team mate and fellow English teacher in Daegu, South Korea. Later, both Mark & Magda, a lovely couple, were colleagues during my time studying in Prague. You might recognise their names in this story. Their advice and knowledge were tremendously helpful during my research. Of course, my friends are much nicer than the despicable characters named after them in these pages. Honestly…

Of course, a special mention must also go to my friend and mentor, Professor John Onians. His ideas and unsurpassed knowledge are always welcomed, and his input into this story was priceless. John is a true legend, and has been an inspiration in my life for many years. I'm not sure why it was so much fun shooting him so often in this story…

Also, a huge shout out to my small but vital BETA team, Michael Rhew and Tim Birmingham. All remaining mistakes are my own.

And finally, as always, a massive thanks to Leslie Moore, my unstintingly supportive wife.

Thank you.

Steven Moore

COPYRIGHT

THE GOLEM OF PRAGUE

First published by **Condor Publishing** in 2018

Printed in Great Britain
by Amazon